DI

When Apples Grew Noses and White Horses Flew

•

Tales of Ti-Jean

When Apples Grew Noses
and White Horses Flew

•

TALES OF TI-JEAN

JAN ANDREWS

Illustrations by

Dušan Petričić

Groundwood Books / House of Anansi Press
Toronto   Berkeley

Text copyright © 2011 by Jan Andrews
Illustrations copyright © 2011 by Dušan Petričić

Published in Canada and the USA in 2011 by Groundwood Books

Groundwood Books / House of Anansi Press
110 Spadina Avenue, Suite 801, Toronto, Ontario M5V 2K4
or c/o Publishers Group West
1700 Fourth Street, Berkeley, CA 94710

We acknowledge for their financial support of our publishing program the Canada Council
for the Arts, the Government of Canada through the Canada Book Fund (CBF)
and the Ontario Arts Council.

 Canada Council **Conseil des Arts**
for the Arts **du Canada**

 ONTARIO ARTS COUNCIL
CONSEIL DES ARTS DE L'ONTARIO

Library and Archives Canada Cataloguing in Publication
Andrews, Jan
When apples grew noses and white horses flew : tales of Ti-Jean / Jan
Andrews ; illustrations by Dušan Petričić.
ISBN 978-0-88899-952-8
1. Ti-Jean (Legendary character) — Juvenile fiction. 2. Children's
stories, Canadian (English). I. Petričić, Dušan II. Title. III. Title:
Tales of Ti-Jean.
PS8551.N37W54 2011   jC813'.54   C2010-905903-4

Cover illustration by Dušan Petričić
The illustrations are in black pencil and Photoshop.
Design by Michael Solomon
Printed and bound in Canada

To Ellis Lynn, who has inspired in so many
children a love of the old tales.

J.A.

For my grandson Uroš, who just learned to walk.

D.P.

Contents

•

A Word About Ti-Jean

As soon as you start going from one of these stories to another, you'll realize Ti-Jean is a hero unlike most others. He turns up in different times and places. He gets married at the end of one tale. He's on a quest for a bride at the beginning of the next. His mother is dead. No, she isn't. It's his father. He's wise, he's foolish. The only thing he isn't ever is rich.

So, you'll be asking, who is he? The answer is he's part of a long, long tradition (a lot like Jack in English fairy tales). He changes because we change and really he's all about us — the difficulties we get into and the adventures we're bound to have. Many, many people have created stories about him over the years. They've told those stories around fires and in logging camps, in countryside and in town. They've remembered those stories — perhaps not quite exactly, but what they have remembered, they've passed on.

What does that say? I think it says that if you have an urge to tell a Ti-Jean story or make one up, you should do it, but you should also be careful to share that story with someone else.

Jan Andrews

Ti-Jean and the Princess
of Tomboso

Cric, crac,
Parli, parlons, parlo.
If you won't listen,
Out you go.

L ÉTAIT UNE FOIS... Which is to say, *There was once...*

There was once a farmer. That farmer had come to the New World from France in a ship with great white sails. He was just like everyone else who had chosen to journey here. He was searching for a better life.

He lived on a narrow strip of land running down to a river. All of the farms in that part of the country were narrow strips. All of them ran down to rivers so everyone could have a proper share of water and an easier way of getting about.

The work of the farm was hard. It did not exactly bring the farmer the riches he had hoped for, but he was content enough. He had three sons, and whenever they were worried about what the future might bring, he always said, "When I came from the Old Country I brought gifts that I have saved for you. When I die, you will have them. When you have the gifts, you'll have nothing to worry about."

Time passed and the farmer grew old. He grew sick and took to his bed. He called his sons to him.

"Go into the barn," he told them. "Far at the back, deep under the hay, you'll find a chest. That chest contains three objects, one for each of you. I'll give you the key now, but if you care about me, you'll wait until I am dead to use it."

The sons did wait. They nursed their father and tended to him. They made sure he had a fine funeral with all of the neighbors to pray for his soul.

At last, however, the funeral was over.

"I believe we can look in the chest now," the oldest son announced.

They went into the barn, all three of them together. They dug into the hay at the back. Sure enough, the chest was there as their father had told them it would be.

The oldest brother put the key in the lock and turned it. The second lifted the lid. The third just watched and waited. His name was Ti-Jean. He wasn't as quick off the mark as the other two. They didn't think much of his chances in the world.

Inside the chest were three objects, just as their father had said. One was a purse, one was a bugle, one was a belt. The objects were not quite the gifts the brothers had been expecting, but when the oldest brother saw his name on the purse, he picked it up.

On the side of the purse was writing.

Every time I open wide, a hundred gold coins are inside.

The oldest brother opened the purse. He could hardly believe his eyes. There were the gold coins all ready to be counted. He opened the purse again. There were more coins.

The brothers knew the money was going to be useful. It was going to be very useful indeed.

The second brother saw his name on the bugle. That had writing on it, too.

Blow one end, the troops appear. Blow the other, the field is clear.

The second brother blew on the bugle. He blew on the narrow end, the mouthpiece.

Outside the barn there was the sound of marching feet and officers shouting orders. The second brother went to the door to look.

"I've never seen so many soldiers in my life," he cried.

His brothers were quite relieved when he blew on the wide end of the bugle and the soldiers disappeared.

Now, of course, the brothers wanted to know about the belt.

Ti-Jean saw his name on it. He picked it up. He looked at the back.

"It says, *Put me on and tell me where. In a minute you'll be there*," he read.

"Where are you going to go?" his brothers asked.

"I want to see the Princess of Tomboso," Ti-Jean replied.

"She's just in a story," his brothers insisted.

"She isn't," said Ti-Jean. "I want to go to the Princess of Tomboso."

With that, he was in the Princess of Tomboso's room. She was sitting on her throne eating an apple. She was very pretty and very surprised to see him.

"Who are you? Why have you come here?" she asked.

"My name is Ti-Jean. I've come for a visit."

The princess looked at him more carefully. She noticed he was not as richly dressed as everyone else who approached her.

"My servants should never have let you enter the palace," she exclaimed.

"Your servants could not stop me," Ti-Jean replied. "I came directly here to where you are."

"Such a thing is not possible."

"It is," said Ti-Jean. "I have a magic belt."

"Show me," she ordered.

"With pleasure."

Ti-Jean showed her the belt. He demonstrated how it worked by having it carry him into a closet and out.

The princess was very interested. She wanted to look more closely.

"Might I touch it?" she asked.

"I would be honored."

"Could I try on the belt, perhaps?"

"You are most welcome," Ti-Jean said.

The princess put on the belt at once. Ti-Jean watched and waited.

The princess ordered the belt to take her to her father's throne room.

The next thing Ti-Jean knew, he was facing the palace guards. They beat him until he was black and blue all over. They marched him through the palace door and left him in a ditch.

Ti-Jean did not want to go home. He did not want to tell his brothers what had happened, but he did not know what else to do, so he set out.

The way was long and perilous. By the time he arrived, his brothers were living much more comfortably, thanks to his oldest brother's purse and the gold coins.

His brothers welcomed him and teased him. They called him a dunderhead and life went on.

Perhaps that would have been the end of it, but Ti-Jean wanted his belt back. He wanted it very much. As well, he kept remembering how pretty the Princess of Tomboso had looked.

Perhaps she did not really mean to steal the belt from me. Perhaps it was really her father's fault, he thought.

He racked his brains and racked his brains until at last he came up with a plan. He went to his oldest brother.

"I was wondering if I could borrow the purse from you," he said.

"The purse? Why would I lend you the purse?"

"Because it's the only way I can get my belt back. If I have the purse, I can buy the belt."

The oldest brother was very doubtful, but Ti-Jean begged and pleaded.

"You must promise you won't let the princess hold the purse," his brother said finally.

"I promise," Ti-Jean answered.

"You must promise you won't even let her touch it."

"I promise! *I promise!*"

The oldest brother was still reluctant, but he agreed.

Ti-Jean set out. He had the purse so he did not have to walk much. Mostly he could afford to ride. He was better dressed than he had been but he still looked like a farmer. He could pay the princess's servants to let him into the palace, though.

This time he came into her room through the door. Once more she was sitting on her throne. Once more she was eating an apple. She was still wearing the belt.

The princess was not pleased to see him. She was not pleased at all.

"I don't want you in my room," she told him.

"I would go in an instant, if you would give me back my belt," Ti-Jean said.

"It's mine. I'm not giving it to anyone," the princess answered.

"Then perhaps I could buy it."

"You wouldn't have enough money."

"I could fill this room with gold coins again and again."

"How could you possibly do that?"

All this while, Ti-Jean had kept the purse in his pocket. Now he took it out. He told the princess how it worked. He produced one hundred gold coins and then another hundred.

The princess looked at him and smiled.

"I would like so much to touch this wonderful purse," she said.

"I don't think you can," said Ti-Jean. "I don't think my brother would like it."

The princess smiled some more. Ti-Jean had never seen anyone so lovely. He forgot his promise. He forgot everything. He let her touch the purse.

"Could I hold it?" she asked him.

He let her.

"Could I try it for myself?" she demanded.

Ti-Jean was a little unsure, but only a little.

"Of course you may try it, but then you must give it back," he said.

"What else would I do?" the princess cried.

She tried the purse once. She tried it twice. Ti-Jean watched and waited.

"I want to go to my father's throne room now," the princess told the belt.

She took the purse with her. Of course she did.

Ti-Jean found himself facing the palace guards again. This time they didn't just beat him and march him through the door. They threw him out the window. He

was so sore that for three days and three nights he could hardly move.

How could he go back to his brothers? How could he admit that the purse was gone? His family was going to be poor again.

Strangely enough, he already had another plan.

"If I just had the bugle," he told his second brother.

"The bugle! Why would I give you the bugle so you can lose that, too?"

"Because with the bugle I will have an army. I can make the princess do whatever I want. I can get the purse. I can get the belt. We will have everything back again."

His brothers did not like the idea, but they could see no other way.

"You must promise you won't let the princess hold the bugle," his second brother said finally.

"I promise," Ti-Jean answered.

"You won't even let her touch it. You won't go near where she can reach it."

"I promise! *I promise!* I'm going to stand outside the palace gates. I'm going to wait for her."

At last, the second brother agreed.

Ti-Jean went back to Tomboso. He stood outside the palace gates. He waited until the Princess of Tomboso came riding forth. She still looked very pretty. She was eating another apple.

Ti-Jean blew on the bugle. The army appeared at once. Ti-Jean commanded the soldiers to point their guns toward the palace walls.

The princess was very frightened, especially when she saw Ti-Jean.

"What is the cause of this?" she demanded.

"I am the cause," Ti-Jean said. "I have come for my purse and my belt and if I do not get them I will order my troops to fire."

"But how could you have an army?" the princess asked.

Ti-Jean was more than happy to explain. He demonstrated how he could send his soldiers away and summon them back to him.

"The instructions are written on the bugle. Blow one end, the troops appear, blow the other, the field is clear," he said.

The princess rode a little closer.

"Show me once more," she begged.

Ti-Jean showed her. The princess came closer still.

"I know that I am in your power," she cried out.

"You are!" said Ti-Jean.

He went to stand beside her. She snatched the bugle from his grasp.

"I believe I must blow on the wide end first," she said.

She sent his troops away.

Ti-Jean had nothing. The princess summoned another army — an army of her own. She ordered the soldiers to march over Ti-Jean until he was flattened. He lay where they left him. He lay unmoving. He lay for seven nights and seven days.

This time he knew he could not go home to his brothers. He crawled away on hands and knees. He crept under hedges and through ditches. He dragged himself through marshes until at last he came to an orchard.

Beneath the trees, apples lay on the ground. By then, Ti-Jean was very hungry.

I'll eat an apple before I die, he thought.

The apples were good so he ate several.

All of a sudden his head seemed so heavy he could hardly hold it up. Something was pulling at it. It kept falling forward.

He ate another apple. The pulling grew stronger. That was because his nose was longer than it had been. His nose was very long indeed.

Death is the only answer to my woes, he decided.

Once more he lay on the ground. He lay there for quite a while.

By then he noticed there were plum trees growing a little farther off.

Why not a plum before I die, he thought.

The plums were good, too. As he ate them, he realized his head was getting lighter.

He reached up. His nose was shorter. He kept eating plums until his nose was back to its normal size.

He was going to go on his way, but it occurred to him that he had met someone who seemed to be quite fond of apples. He gathered up some apples to put in one pocket. He gathered up some plums to put in another.

He headed back to the Princess of Tomboso's palace.

He did not go to the front door. He went to the servants' entrance. He told the cook that these were special apples and that she should send them up to the princess immediately. She should tell the princess the apples must be eaten quickly or they would lose their flavor.

The cook put the apples in a fancy basket. She sent them to the princess's room.

The princess was pleased. She started eating the apples at once. She ate far more than Ti-Jean had eaten. Her nose grew so long that it touched the ground, even when she was standing up.

The king was distraught. He summoned the royal doctors. None of them could find a cure. Doctors came from all the surrounding lands. No one had seen an illness like it. No one could help the princess.

She sobbed and she raged. It made no difference.

Ti-Jean watched and waited. He was good at watching and waiting.

When the doctors stopped arriving, he went to the cook again. He suggested that he might have a cure.

Before he knew it, he was standing in front of the king's throne. The king sent him to the princess. She was not sitting on her throne this time. She was lying on her bed. Her nose stretched down to her toes.

"Why can't you leave me alone?" she cried.

"I could," said Ti-Jean. "But I think I can help you. I can do what others have not."

"Then help me," said the princess. "Help me as quickly as you can."

"I'd like my payment first," said Ti-Jean. "I'd like my bugle back."

"Who cares about your old bugle?"

"I do."

"Why should I part with it?"

"Because if you don't, I will leave at once."

"All right," said the princess. "But you can only have the bugle. You will find it in the drawer."

Ti-Jean got the bugle.

"You remember what I can do with this, don't you?" he said.

"Of course I do," the princess answered. "Can't you hurry?"

"Well," said Ti-Jean, "I think you should try this plum. I think, with this plum, you will discover..."

Already the princess's nose was shrinking, but it shrank only to her knees.

"Give me another plum," she ordered.

"I'd like my purse back first," he told her.

"I don't want to give it to you."

"Perhaps you will get used to your nose then. It won't drag on the ground any longer. Although when it comes to finding a husband..."

"The purse is in that other drawer."

"Thank you," Ti-Jean said. "I am most grateful. I'm sure this second plum will also help."

The plum did help. The princess's nose stretched only to her waist now.

"I want my nose its proper length," she cried.

"Then we must also discuss the matter of my belt."

The princess did discuss it. She discussed it angrily, but at last she gave in.

Ti-Jean put on the belt. He held out a third plum. The princess's nose shrank until it reached only to her chest.

"It's not enough," she screamed.

But it was too late. Already Ti-Jean was gone. He was back in his own home with his brothers. He was telling them about his adventures.

"I don't think the princess will steal anyone else's belongings," he said.

His brothers congratulated him because they could see that in the end he had been quite smart. Together, they all settled down to enjoy life once more. They had plenty of money. The farm prospered. They took turns traveling wherever they wanted.

Sometimes, on a Saturday evening when the work was done and they needed entertaining, they blew on the bugle so they could watch the troops march back and forth, but they never again had to use them. They had no cause.

> *Sac-à-tabac,*
> *Sac-à-tabi.*
> *The story's ended.*
> *C'est fini.*

TI-JEAN THE MARBLE PLAYER

Ti-Jean here, Ti-Jean there,
Ti-Jean, Ti-Jean everywhere.

ERE'S SOMETHING you should know about Ti-Jean. He loved to play at marbles. He would have played all day and all night if he had not had to work for his father in the fields.

Because he played marbles so often, he got better and better at it. By the time he was a young man, no one could beat him. He won every single game.

But he still had to work. So it was that one summer morning his father sent him out to hoe the turnips.

Ti-Jean was bending over, hoeing as hard as he could, when all of a sudden a little man popped up in front of him — a very little man indeed. The little man was dressed in red from head to toe. He even had a red tuque on his head.

Ti-Jean had been well brought up. He knew his manners.

"Good day to you," he said.

"Good day to you," said the little man.

"Is there something I can do for you?" Ti-Jean asked.

"I'm here to play marbles with you."

Ti-Jean's eyes lit up, but he shook his head.

"I can't take time off from my work to play marbles. My father will be angry," he replied.

"I only want to play one game," said the little man. "Your father might not be angry with you anyway, for if you beat me, I will give you whatever you wish."

"And if I should lose?" said Ti-Jean.

"You will have to do whatever I ask of you."

A wish seemed like a good thing to try for. Ti-Jean

thought how long it had been since anyone had beaten him.

"I don't see how one game can do any harm," he said.

The little man reached into his pocket. He pulled out a bag of marbles. Right there in the field, they began to play.

Ti-Jean won. He won easily.

"You can tell me your wish now," the little man said.

"Maybe I should know your name first," said Ti-Jean.

"It's Bonnet Rouge. Red Cap, for my red hat."

"Well, Monsieur Bonnet Rouge, you see that field next to this one? My father has told me over and over that it would be just the place for dairy cattle. I'd like it filled with milk cows and I'd like it done by morning," said Ti-Jean.

"A promise is a promise," said Bonnet Rouge.

Sure enough, when Ti-Jean woke up the next morning, he saw a sea of horns. The milk cows were in the field. Of course, he had to tell his father how it had happened. He had to explain what he had done.

His father was pleased enough with the cows, but he gave Ti-Jean a warning.

"You're a generous lad," he said. "Plenty of others would have wished for something just for themselves. Still, that was a risk you took. You could have lost and then who knows what might have occurred. Cows or no cows, I don't want you gambling on wishes any more."

That day, he sent Ti-Jean to hoe potatoes. Ti-Jean

hardly had the hoe in his hands when Bonnet Rouge popped up again.

"It's only fair I should have my chance at winning," he declared.

"What will the arrangements be today, then?" Ti-Jean asked.

"They will be as before," said Bonnet Rouge.

Ti-Jean did not forget his father's warning. But he thought of the cattle and of how easily he had won.

"Surely one more game can't do any harm," he said.

Again Bonnet Rouge reached into his pocket and took out the bag of marbles. Again, right there in the field, the two of them played. Again Ti-Jean was the winner.

"What will you have now?" Bonnet Rouge asked.

"You see that other field, where the grass is greenest? My father has always said that would be the best place in the world for horses. I want it filled with horses — fine ones — and I want it done by morning."

"A promise is a promise," said Bonnet Rouge.

Sure enough, when Ti-Jean woke he could see that the promise had been kept. The field was filled with horses. They were racing and prancing. They were tossing their manes and stamping their feet.

His father guessed what had happened.

"Two risks are enough," he said. And he set Ti-Jean to cleaning out the stable.

Ti-Jean had hardly been at work for a minute when Bonnet Rouge appeared again.

"You must let me have one more try," he insisted.

"Will the arrangements be the same as before?" asked Ti-Jean.

"They will," said Bonnet Rouge.

Ti-Jean thought of those cows. He thought of those horses. He thought of his father's warning, but he also thought of how easily he had won before.

"One game and that's the last," he said.

Out came the bag of marbles from Bonnet Rouge's pocket. Right there in the stable, they played.

Bonnet Rouge won. He won easily.

"What do I have to give you?" Ti-Jean asked.

"You must come to where I live one hundred leagues beyond the setting sun," said Bonnet Rouge. "If I do not see you there in a year and a day, your life will be forfeit."

With that, Bonnet Rouge was gone.

Ti-Jean went to tell his father he had played and lost.

"What is the price you must pay?" his father asked.

"I must go to where Bonnet Rouge lives, one hundred leagues beyond the setting sun. I must visit him in a year and a day or I will lose my life," Ti-Jean replied.

"Would that you had listened to me, my poor Ti-Jean," his father cried.

Ti-Jean began to ask everyone he met about Bonnet Rouge, but no one had heard of him. The days turned into weeks and the weeks into months. The horses and the cattle prospered, but Ti-Jean grew sadder and sadder.

He waited through the falling of the leaves. He waited

through the bitter winter cold. He waited until the snow was gone and the ice had melted. He saw that the time for hoeing turnips and potatoes was approaching.

With a heavy heart, he set out.

He traveled by road, he traveled by canoe along the rivers. He went along the sea shore and through fishing villages. He went through the forests. He came upon the empty shanties where the loggers worked in winter cutting down the trees.

He did not know how far he journeyed. He knew only that a year and a day would soon be past.

At last he came upon a track so overgrown that it seemed no one could have stepped upon it for a very long time.

For many days he saw only forest creatures—squirrels, mink, rabbits, sometimes even a moose.

Finally, one evening, he found himself in front of a small hut. When he knocked, an old woman opened the door. She seemed very surprised to see him.

"No one has come to my hut in more than a hundred years," she said. "What brings you here?"

"I am searching for Bonnet Rouge," Ti-Jean told her.

"Bonnet Rouge is my brother," the old woman exclaimed.

"If Bonnet Rouge is your brother, surely you will be able to help me find him," Ti-Jean said.

"I fear I will not," the old woman answered. "I am the youngest in the family. He does not come to see me."

"Is there nothing you can tell me?" Ti-Jean cried.

"There is nothing I can tell you, but we have a sister," said the old woman. "She is two hundred years older than I am. She lives some distance beyond here. He may have visited her."

"Show me how to get to her, I beg you."

"I will show you," the old woman said. "But I will show you in the morning. For tonight I will give you a place to rest and food to eat before you go on."

Ti-Jean went into the old woman's hut. He ate well and he slept. In the morning, she gave him a pair of boots made of steel.

"Put these boots on and walk to the southwest. They will carry you to my sister," she told him. "But as soon as you arrive at her hut, you must take the boots off. You must say to them, 'Boots, go on your way,' so they will return to me."

Ti-Jean thanked the old woman. He put on the boots and set off. He walked for several more days.

He was almost ready to give up when he came upon another hut. The boots stopped in front of the door.

Before he knocked, he remembered what the first old woman had told him. He took the boots off his feet.

"Boots, go on your way," he ordered, and he watched them march away.

Just as the first old woman had said, an even older woman lived here.

"Why have you come? What are you seeking?" she asked.

"Your sister told me you would know how to find Bonnet Rouge," Ti-Jean answered.

"Bonnet Rouge! I have not seen him for three hundred years."

"I must find him or I will lose my life," Ti-Jean insisted.

"I will do what I can to help you. Listen! I have another sister. She is one hundred years older than Bonnet Rouge. She knows everything about our family."

"Show me how to get to her, I beg you," Ti-Jean cried.

"I will. But I will show you in the morning. For tonight you must let me give you a place to rest and food to eat."

Ti-Jean went into the second old woman's hut. He ate well and he slept. In the morning, she, too, brought him a pair of boots, but these boots were made of silver.

"The boots will take you to my older sister," she told him. "Remember, though, as soon as you arrive, you must take the boots off. You must say to them, 'Boots, go on your way,' so that they may return to me."

Ti-Jean thanked the second old woman. He promised he would send the boots back to her and he set off.

The boots of silver traveled very quickly. In no time at all he was standing in front of a hut so old that it was covered with moss.

He went to knock, but then he remembered he must take off the boots.

"Boots, go on your way," he said, and they marched back.

36

Now he met a woman who was so old she was almost bent double.

"You must be looking for someone of much importance to you," she said. "It is six hundred years since anyone came by here."

"I am looking for Bonnet Rouge. I have met your two sisters. They have told me you can help me find him."

"Bonnet Rouge!" said the old woman. "You do not wish to see Bonnet Rouge. He brings only trouble to all he meets."

"But if I do not meet him, the worst will come to me. If I do not meet him, I will lose my life," Ti-Jean cried out. He told the third old woman all that had happened.

"You are right, you must find him," she agreed. "I will help you but come in, rest, and let me give you food and drink, for you have much toil and misery ahead."

Ti-Jean went into the old woman's hut. He stayed for three nights and two days. Before dawn on the third day, the old woman came to him carrying a golden ball.

"The ball will guide you," she told him. "It will lead you to a lake. If you wait by the lake, you will see three pigeons. They will circle the lake three times. Each one will drop a feather. They are my brother's daughters. Every day they take the form of pigeons so that they may fly to the lake and bathe. The feathers are their clothes. The one who looks the oldest and dirtiest is the one who is the youngest and prettiest. You must find her

feather and keep it. You must tell her you will give it to her only if she will help you."

Ti-Jean thanked the old woman. The golden ball began to roll ahead of him. All he had to do was follow.

At last, it stopped by a lake. Ti-Jean hid among the reeds.

Quite soon he saw three pigeons flying. They circled the lake three times. They each dropped a feather and then dived down to bathe.

Ti-Jean could see well that one of the pigeons looked older and dirtier and less pleasing than the other two. He went to her feather and picked it up.

In about an hour, the pigeons began to search for their feathers. The two oldest found theirs and flew away. The youngest was left alone.

"Where are my clothes? Oh, where are my clothes?" she cried.

"I have them," said Ti-Jean, stepping out to where she could see him.

"Then you must give them back."

"I will do so gladly, but you must promise you will take me to your father."

"I cannot, for he will be so angry," she replied.

"If you cannot take me to your father, then I am sorry."

"But I must have my clothes. I must."

She argued and she argued. When she saw Ti-Jean would not give in, she said, "I will tell you what to do but you must understand that we cannot go to meet my father together. If he knows that I have brought you, he will kill us both."

"I understand," said Ti-Jean.

"Then follow me until we are almost at the castle. I will go in the front door but you must go to the side. You must knock three times. My mother will answer. Tell her you have a message for my father and she will let you in."

This was enough for Ti-Jean. He gave her back her feather.

As she took it, he saw she was a princess — the most beautiful in all the world.

"I hope I will see you again," he said.

"You will," said the princess, "because again you will need my help. Your troubles are only just beginning. My father is going to give you some tasks. There are two things you must remember. First, you must always make him believe the tasks are easy for you. Second, if he should give you a choice you must always choose the object that is the oldest and dirtiest."

"I will remember," said Ti-Jean.

They began to walk toward the castle. Ti-Jean went to the side door. He knocked three times. He said he had come with a message. The princess's mother let him in.

He had hardly stepped inside when he saw Bonnet Rouge coming toward him carrying an ax.

"You have arrived just in time. I was about to set out to take your life," said Bonnet Rouge.

He did not seem glad to see Ti-Jean. He did not welcome him in any way.

"I will give you a bed of nails to sleep on," he announced.

Ti-Jean was shocked, but he remembered what the princess had told him.

"A bed of nails will be perfect for me," he said.

Of course, the bed was not perfect. It was most uncomfortable. Still, in the morning when Bonnet Rouge asked him how he had slept, Ti-Jean said he had slept very well.

"That is good," said Bonnet Rouge, "for today I will

set you to work. Behind the barn there is a field that has not yet been prepared for planting. You must cut down the trees, till the soil and sow the seed, before the setting of the sun."

He held out two axes. One was new and shining, the other old and rusted.

Ti-Jean did not hesitate.

"The old one will be the best for me," he declared.

He went out to the field and set to work, but by noon he had cut down no more than six trees. The task appeared so hopeless that he believed he might as well give up.

He stretched out on the earth there.

I did not sleep in the night, he thought. I will sleep now and accept whatever Bonnet Rouge will do to me.

He had not been sleeping long when the princess came to him.

"Why are you sleeping when the job is not finished?" she asked.

"The job is too much for me. I cannot accomplish even a hundredth of it," Ti-Jean said.

"You can do it with my help." The princess went to the ax and touched it.

"Ax, cut down the trees," she ordered.

The ax began to cut the trees at once. In no time they had all been felled and piled around the edges of the field.

"Earth, set to work," the princess commanded.

The earth began to till itself. In less than an hour, the field had been plowed and the seeds had been sown.

"You must go now to my father," the princess told Ti-Jean. "You must tell him the task is done but you must be careful. He will suspect that I have helped you and he will watch me. Do not try to speak to me again. Wait in your room until you hear my knock. Let me in so that I can tell you how to succeed tomorrow as well."

Ti-Jean went to Bonnet Rouge. Bonnet Rouge was angry. He was very angry indeed.

"The next task will be harder," he shouted.

"But this one was so easy," Ti-Jean said.

On this night, Bonnet Rouge gave him a good mattress. Ti-Jean was so tired that he fell asleep at once. He slept like a log.

At midnight, the princess came knocking on the door, but he did not hear her. She knocked and she knocked and then she went away.

At dawn, Bonnet Rouge came to wake him.

"I will give you your second task," he said. "On the

castle grounds there is a lake. Seven years ago, my wife was rowing upon it in her boat. She dropped her golden ring into the water. You must empty the lake and find the ring and you must do it before the setting of the sun."

He held out two buckets. One was brand new. The other looked as if it might have holes in it. Still, Ti-Jean remembered what the princess had told him.

"The old bucket will be the best for me," he said.

He took it and set off whistling. Bonnet Rouge was even angrier.

How would Ti-Jean know that he must choose the older bucket? he asked himself.

Ti-Jean was happy. He thought he knew what to do. He reached the lake and touched the bucket.

"Bucket, drain the lake," he said.

The bucket did nothing.

"Lake, drain yourself," Ti-Jean commanded.

The lake did not move.

Ti-Jean filled the bucket as best he could, but there was nowhere for the water to go and soon it started running back.

The lake was not shrinking. It was not shrinking at all.

Ti-Jean called for the princess but she did not come to him. He knew then what had happened.

I have upset her. I must have slept so soundly I did not hear her knock, he thought.

Once more he decided that he might as well lie down and rest.

Late in the afternoon he woke with a start. He saw that the water in the lake was just as it had been. He saw that no one had come to help him.

Desperately, he began to walk around the lake's shores. He even thought about throwing himself in so he would drown.

The princess was watching. She pitied him. She went to him again.

"How is it that you call for my help now, when in the night you would not even speak to me?" she asked.

"I could not help it. I was so tired. I did not hear you," Ti-Jean explained.

"Very well," said the princess. "Let us see what we can do."

She took the old bucket and she held it.

"Bucket, empty the lake," she said.

The bucket went to work at once. In minutes, there was not a drop of water to be seen.

"Ring, come here," the princess called.

At once, the ring landed at Ti-Jean's feet.

"Now," said the princess, "you must listen even more carefully. Tomorrow my father will give you one last task. If you succeed you will be free of him, but if you do not you will have to stay here as his prisoner and serve as his slave forever. Tonight when I knock at your door, be certain that you answer. Let me in so that I may tell you what you must do."

Ti-Jean promised he would. He returned to Bonnet Rouge to give him the ring. Bonnet Rouge was so angry he started to shake.

"My daughter must have helped you," he said.

"No," said Ti-Jean. "The task was easy."

"My daughter helped you but I will put a stop to that. Tomorrow I will see to it that she remains locked in her room."

That night, Ti-Jean did not even lie down. He was so determined to stay awake.

At midnight, he heard the princess knocking and calling out to him. He answered her at once.

"Tomorrow," she told him, "my father will ask you to build a barn and to thatch it with feathers. Here are my magic wand and my magic whistle. I will lend them to you. You only have to touch the hammer with the wand and it will do the work for you. The whistle will summon the birds. My father will give you a gun to kill them but you will not have to do this. Simply touch the gun with the wand and that will be enough. Remember, whatever my father offers you, choose that which is the oldest and dirtiest. Remember also that I cannot help you anymore."

Ti-Jean thanked the princess. He thanked her very much.

In the morning, Bonnet Rouge came to him at the first light of day.

"You must build me a barn and thatch it with feathers and you must do it before the sun sets," he said.

"That does not seem so very much," Ti-Jean was careful to reply.

Bonnet Rouge laughed.

"But today you will work alone," he roared.

He held out two hammers. Ti-Jean took the oldest and the dirtiest. Bonnet Rouge held out two guns.

"The old one will be the best for me," Ti-Jean announced.

He went off whistling once again. Immediately, he set to work.

"Hammer, build the barn," he ordered, touching it with the wand.

The barn was built in less than an hour.

Now for the roof, Ti-Jean thought, as he put the magic whistle to his lips.

With the first notes, a flock of birds came flying. There were so many of all shapes and sizes that they darkened the sky. As the flock passed over the barn, Ti-Jean touched the gun with the wand. From each of the birds fell seven feathers. The feathers were enough to thatch the roof and more besides.

When Bonnet Rouge heard that the barn had been built and thatched just as he had demanded, his anger was terrible. He went red all over. He shook with rage from head to foot. He tried to make Ti-Jean tell him who had helped him, but Ti-Jean was faithful. Over and over, he insisted that the tasks had not been hard.

"You have beaten me," Bonnet Rouge said finally. "Tomorrow I will let you leave."

Ti-Jean went to his room, but he lay wakeful. Just at midnight, he heard the princess's knock. He let her in and gave her back the magic wand and the magic whistle. He thanked her yet again.

"It is not time to thank me yet," she told him. "Tomorrow my father will not set you free. He will kill you. If you wish to remain alive, you must leave at once."

"How will I do that?" Ti-Jean asked.

"I will go to the barn and I will free the white mare. When she comes to your window, you must jump

upon her back. Go in the direction of the rising sun. My father will never be able to catch you. The mare flies on the wings of the wind. She will carry you home, but remember, when you arrive, you must say to her, 'Mare, go back to your mistress,' so she will return to me."

"This I will do, I promise," Ti-Jean said.

He went and waited by the window. Very soon the mare appeared. He saw her coat of shining whiteness and he leapt upon her back. He said goodbye to the princess.

"You have saved my life and I am more grateful to you than I can say," he said.

"Perhaps I will see you again," the princess answered.

"I hope so! Oh, I hope so," Ti-Jean replied.

He flew then like the wind. He came to the home of his parents.

"Mare, go back to your mistress," he commanded, and the mare sped off.

His parents were so happy to see him that they gave him a great welcome. They had a party and invited the neighbors to come. The cows and the horses were still there. They had grown and flourished. Their coats gleamed in the sun. Ti-Jean's father could not help himself. He was pleased with his son despite all the trouble he had brought.

As for Ti-Jean, he still played marbles. But he was more careful who he played with from then on.

Sac-à-tabac,
Sac-à-tabi.
The story's ended.
C'est fini.

How Ti-Jean Became a Fiddler

Ti-Jean up, Ti-Jean down,
Ti-Jean all around the town.
Sometimes wrong and sometimes right,
Ti-Jean, Ti-Jean, man of might.

T WASN'T ONLY farmers who came to
the New World in those ships with
great white sails. Rich people came as
well. They were called *les seigneurs* —
the lords — and they set themselves up
to live in style. The king of France, who was also their
king, gave them land to rule over. Each piece of land
was called *une seigneurie*. It was divided up and rented
out to people who were not so well off. In a way, each
seigneurie was like a kingdom unto itself.

That's where this story begins. It begins on one of
those seigneuries.

Now it happened that this seigneur had a daughter,
and that daughter was very clever. Life was not then as
it is now, of course. In those days, when it came time for

a girl to marry, her father chose her husband. That's just how it was.

The seigneur believed that if his daughter was clever, she would need to marry a clever man. He sent his servants near and far to post messages saying that anyone who could talk to her in such a way that she could find no answer would be the chosen one. Anyone who failed would be thrown into prison and would have to stay there for a year and a day. That's because the seigneur did not want his daughter's time wasted with men who had no chance.

Where was Ti-Jean in all of this? He was living three days' journey off with his mother and his two older brothers. His father was a voyageur. That meant he spent most of his time working in the fur trade in the lands to the west. He left in the spring as soon as the ice on the rivers melted. He did not come back again until late in the fall.

Because their father was not home, Ti-Jean's brothers took it upon themselves to give the orders. Not to Ti-Jean's mother. She was not the kind of person to be ordered about by her own sons. They ordered Ti-Jean around, though. They treated him like a servant. They made him fetch and carry and do more than his share of the work.

They never took him with them when they went anywhere. Mostly he did not mind because he liked being home. He helped his mother in the kitchen. He worked with her in the garden. He looked after the chickens. He fed the pigs and milked the cows.

By going places, his brothers heard the news. One day they heard about the seigneur and his daughter. They came back from the market talking of nothing else.

They decided that this was their opportunity to improve themselves.

"You're more likely to be thrown into prison," their mother told them, but they did not listen to her.

The very next morning, they dressed themselves in their best, mounted their horses and set out.

"Would you like to have gone with them this time?" Ti-Jean's mother asked.

"It seems like an adventure," Ti-Jean said.

"I have this feeling your brothers are going to need you," his mother told him.

"In that case, I'll go for sure," Ti-Jean replied.

He took the not-so-good horse. It was all that was left, but he thought it was good enough for him. He traveled as quickly as he could until he could see his brothers in the distance. After that he hung back because he was sure they would try to chase him away.

Late in the day, they came to a town. His brothers had money. They got themselves rooms at the inn. Ti-Jean was not quite certain how he would manage.

Perhaps if I go to the kitchen, he thought, they'll let me work for food and a place to sleep.

The cook looked him up and she looked him down.

"Can you carry water?" she asked.

"I can," said Ti-Jean.

"Can you bring in the wood so I can keep my stove going?"

"I can," said Ti-Jean. "I can carry water and bring in the wood. I can chop vegetables and watch the meat. I can even wash the dishes because my mother taught me. I will work quickly and I will work hard."

At that, the cook agreed. Ti-Jean was true to his word, too. He worked as fast and as hard as he could. He brought in the wood. He brought in the water. He chopped great piles of vegetables. He watched the meat. He washed one mountain of dishes after another. He did not stop until everything that needed doing was done.

The cook gave him food in plenty and a place to sleep in the stable. She made sure his horse was fed as well.

In the morning when Ti-Jean was about to go on again, she offered him a gift.

"I've never known anyone so cheerful and so willing," she told him. "Here's a napkin for you. If ever you're hungry, open it up and tell it what you'd like to eat. Whatever you ask for will appear."

"Thank you indeed," said Ti-Jean.

All day he followed his brothers again. By nightfall they had reached another town. It was the same as the day before. Ti-Jean's brothers rented rooms for themselves at the inn. Ti-Jean had nowhere to go. Still, this time he did not have to wonder how he would manage. He went to the kitchen right off.

The cook asked him the same kinds of questions. He gave the same answers.

This inn was even busier. He worked even harder than he had before. All the servants were amazed at what he did for them. They made sure he had a good supper so he was not hungry. They made sure he had a place to sleep in the stable so he could rest.

In the morning they all gathered together at the kitchen door to see him off.

"You really helped us. You made the whole evening go better than it has ever gone," they said.

They told him they had a gift for him. The gift turned out to be a bottle.

"If you're thirsty and you want something to drink, all

you have to do is pull out the cork and give your orders. You'll have what you need and more," they explained.

"Thank you indeed," said Ti-Jean.

This was the day when he and his brothers would come to where the seigneur lived. They arrived about noon. The seigneur's servants told Ti-Jean's brothers they would have to return the next morning. His brothers went off to find another inn. Ti-Jean thought maybe he would like a change.

He went to find the seigneur's gardener.

"If I would work the rest of the day for you, would you give me supper and a place to sleep?" he asked.

"Do you know how to set seeds?" the gardener asked him.

"I do," said Ti-Jean.

"Can you plant out seedlings and water them carefully?"

"I can," said Ti-Jean. "I can set seeds and plant out seedlings. I can weed and rake and hoe. I can even prune trees, for my mother taught me. I will work quickly and I will work hard."

Again he was true to his word. He worked the rest of the day for the gardener. He did everything he was asked. He smiled all the time because being in the garden made him think of his mother. He set seeds and he planted out seedlings. He weeded and raked and hoed and pruned.

"You're the best helper I've ever had," the gardener told him.

The gardener was so grateful that he not only gave Ti-Jean a meal, he gave him a bed in his own house.

"I wish you could stay longer," the gardener said in the morning. "But since you can't, I'll give you a gift."

He brought out a violin — a fiddle. It was old and shiny and brown.

"Is that for me?" Ti-Jean asked.

"It is," said the gardener. "If ever you're in need of singing and dancing, all you have to do is put the bow to the strings and the fiddle will play."

Ti-Jean was overjoyed. A fiddle was precious. It made people happy.

"Thank you indeed," he said.

He tucked the fiddle under his arm and he went to the seigneur's great house. He did not have any trouble getting in. There were so many others entering as well. Some of them had come because they wanted to try to marry the seigneur's daughter. Some of them had come because they wanted to watch. Ti-Jean was able to hide among them easily enough.

The seigneur's daughter sat in one big chair and the seigneur and his wife sat on two others. The contestants came up one by one. Ti-Jean's brothers were not at the head of the line by a long shot.

Ti-Jean could not believe what was talked about. He listened to discussions about the sun and the moon and the stars and the planets. He heard debates about faraway countries and far-off times. He heard of things he had never even thought of.

The seigneur's daughter answered every question. She had something to add to every topic.

He could see his brothers were beginning to look pale. They were beginning to look very pale indeed.

At last the eldest's turn came. He asked the seigneur's daughter to name all the trees in the forest. She looked at him as if he was a maggot. She reeled off the names at once.

The oldest brother was thrown in prison.

The second brother stood before her. He tried to talk to her about the best times for planting cabbages.

He was thrown in prison as well.

By that time, Ti-Jean was angry. He pushed his way through the crowd. He stood in front of the seigneur's daughter and shook his fist at her.

"You should be ashamed of yourself," he shouted. "The contest is not fair. The contest is cruel. You should think of the suffering you're causing."

The seigneur's daughter was used to people bowing to her. She was used to them asking how they could please her.

She went red with anger. Ti-Jean kept talking and talking, telling her how wrong she was.

She wanted to answer but she could not. She tried to make her mouth move but it seemed her lips were glued together. She sputtered but did not speak.

People began to laugh. The seigneur knew he must put a stop to what was happening.

"I am afraid you will have to marry this man," he said.

"That's not what I want," said Ti-Jean. "I want to be with my brothers. I want to go to prison."

"You're sure?" asked the seigneur.

"I am certain."

"Take him to the prison!" the seigneur decreed.

Ti-Jean was pushed down the prison stairs. He went where his brothers had gone. Of course, they were not alone. The prison cells were full and all of the men were starving.

"I'll put an end to that," Ti-Jean announced.

He brought out the napkin the cook had given him.

"What would you like to eat?" he demanded.

"Roast chicken with potatoes, vegetables and gravy," said his oldest brother.

"Cake with cream for dessert," said the other.

"Everyone can choose whatever he wants," Ti-Jean announced.

"Fish, well cooked."

"Venison, finely seasoned."

"Pie with apples such as my grandmother baked."

A feast appeared before them.

"What is a feast without wine?" Ti-Jean cried.

He brought out his bottle. He ordered it to fill itself with good wine over and over again.

"A feast is nothing without music," he declared.

He brought out his fiddle. He put the bow to the strings and began to play.

All the prisoners started to dance. Their feet beat out the rhythm. They began to laugh and sing as well.

The noise grew louder and louder. It grew so loud that it reached the ears of the seigneur. It grew so loud that he was frightened.

"Take food to the prisoners," he ordered his servants.

His servants took a great cauldron of pea soup. They would have given the soup to the prisoners, but all of a sudden the servants found they had joined in the dancing — and the singing and the laughter, too.

The soup was spilled. The noise from the prison grew louder.

The seigneur decided he must go down himself and put a stop to it. He tried to shout the order but the prisoners only laughed harder, for the seigneur was dancing as well. He was dancing as if his life depended on it.

The seigneur's wife could also hear the commotion.

When the seigneur did not return, she decided she must go and see.

Down to the prison she went. She might have been surprised to find him flinging his arms about and jigging, but before she knew it she was flinging her arms about and jigging, too.

There had never been a party like it. Everyone was enjoying themselves but everyone was also growing tired.

It was the seigneur who understood first that nothing would change unless Ti-Jean stopped playing.

"If you put an end to the music, I will give you half my seigneurie to rule over as well as my daughter's hand in marriage," he announced.

"What I want most is for all of the prisoners to be freed," Ti-Jean insisted.

"It will be done, I promise. It will be done this instant. See, the prison gates are open. The prisoners can go to their homes. They can go anywhere."

"I will stop playing," Ti-Jean agreed.

As soon as he did, the singing and dancing were over. All of the prisoners rushed to leave. All except Ti-Jean's brothers. They stayed to thank Ti-Jean for rescuing them.

"It was our mother who sent me," Ti-Jean said.

He went then to meet the seigneur's daughter.

"I do not want to rule my half of the seigneurie in the old way," he told her father. "I want to find a way that is better. Anyway, I believe your daughter and I should get to know each other before the marriage takes place."

"You are a wise man after all," the seigneur told him.

It seemed his daughter agreed. She went with Ti-Jean happily to meet his mother. By the time the visit was over, she and Ti-Jean did indeed know each other much better. And so the wedding was arranged. Once they were married, Ti-Jean and his bride ruled over their half of the seigneurie together.

They gave much thought to looking after people and helping as they could. Of one thing you can be certain. There was plenty of music and there was plenty of singing and dancing and laughter. Ti-Jean played his fiddle often, although he was always careful about knowing when to stop.

Never again did he try to make it so that his wife would be struck dumb. Why would he? He liked listening to her talk. He thought she had much to tell him. He thought there was much he could learn.

It is true, however, that sometimes both of them were

silent. That is because they loved each other deeply and truly and more than words can tell.

Encore une fois, c'est la fin. Once more it is the end.

> *Ti-Jean here,*
> *Ti-Jean there,*
> *Ti-Jean, Ti-Jean everywhere.*
> *When days are dark,*
> *When work is long,*
> *Ti-Jean, Ti-Jean helps us on.*
> *Always he finds magic.*
> *Always he will dream.*
> *Always he takes journeys,*
> *Fights his way through others' schemes.*
> *Ti-Jean brought from long ago,*
> *Ti-Jean for today.*
> *Ti-Jean, friend to all of us,*
> *À Ti-Jean, dites Hooray!*

A Note on Sources

"Ti-Jean and the Princess of Tomboso" originates as "The Princess of Tomboso" in *The Golden Phoenix and Other French-Canadian Fairy Tales* by Marius Barbeau, retold by Michael Hornyansky (Toronto: Oxford University Press, 1958). It represents a wonderful example of how stories travel, because although the tale clearly has its roots in the oral traditions of France, it was first collected in Canada from Ojibwa tellers who, presumably, had heard it from the voyageurs.

"Ti-Jean the Marble Player" comes from *Ti-Jean: Contes Acadiens* by Melvin Gallant (Moncton: Editions d'Acadie, 1973). There the story is called "Bonnet Rouge." Melvin Gallant is from Prince Edward Island and has worked steadfastly to ensure the preservation of Acadian literary and folk traditions.

"How Ti-Jean Became a Fiddler" is from *Mille ans de contes — Québec, textes choisis et commentés par Cécile Gagnon* (Toulouse: Editions Milan, 1996). *Mille ans de contes* is a series, embracing many themes. Cécile Gagnon is one of French Canada's much-loved children's writers. She calls the story "Ti-Jean, le violoneux."

In working with these stories, I have sought consistently to find means to root them more firmly in the North American landscape and heritage. The stories have been with us a long time now. All have come to us from Europe, but it seemed they might no longer need the kings and queens that are so much a part of European history. The stories might need the history that is our own.